The Shadow Moon

A Title From Beneath

THE STORY TREE

For
Ruth
⤳H

I hope that you enjoy
The Story Tree!!!
⤳H
SA Bergquist

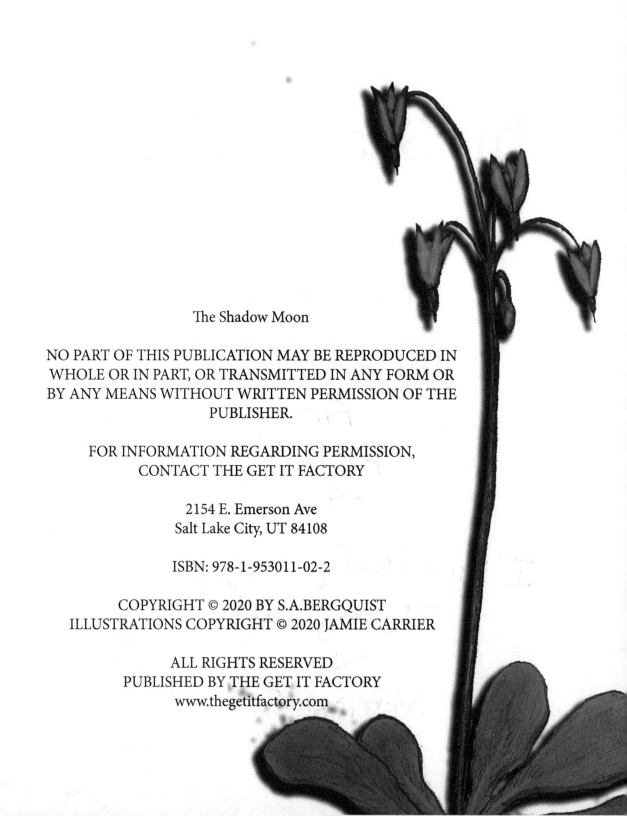

The Shadow Moon

FOR INFORMATION REGARDING PERMISSION, CONTACT THE GET IT FACTORY

2154 E. Emerson Ave
Salt Lake City, UT 84108

ISBN: 978-1-953011-02-2

PUBLISHED BY THE GET IT FACTORY
www.thegetitfactory.com

THE
SHADOW MOON

S.A. BERGQUIST

Illustrations By:
Jamie Carrier

The Get It Factory

For my children.

Without them I would never have met Dylan, Drew, Svea, and...

"Always be on the lookout for the presence of wonder"
- E.B. White

"Look deep into nature, and then you will understand everything better"

- Albert Einstein

It had been early spring with the snow still covering the ground the night that Molly and Sal were born in a den nestled in a stand of pine near a cabin in the mountains of western Montana.

The powdery blue glow of a full moon reflected off the rocks and trees and river that night, some weeks ago, and tonight the full moon...the Shadow Moon...had returned.

Moonlight washed in through the entrance of the den and fell on the faces of the girls sleeping quietly side by side. Their mother, Rosie, smiled down at them and thought of the many things they would see and experience and learn on this special night, their very first night leaving the den.

Gently she put a paw on the shoulder of each girl and nudged them.

"Time to get up girls," she said. "The sun is down."

Now, to be clear, Rosie and her girls, Molly and Sal, lived in a den in the mountains, had paws instead of hands, and woke when the sun went down because...they were racoons! And the rambunctious young racoons had been very excited about this night for quite some time.

They both woke instantly and looked at their mother with wide grins. They rose quickly and followed her to the entrance of the den. They stopped there and looked in wonder at the luminous landscape spread out before them.

"Oh, Mama," said Molly. "It's so beautiful!"
"It's amazing Mama!" exclaimed Sal.

And...they were right. What lay before them was indeed beautiful and amazing and much more.

The landscape, normally seen sharp and clear in the bright light of day, was transformed by the Shadow Moon, suspended high in a cloudless sky, into a magical vista of muted color and shimmering rock and velvet shadow that spread into the quiet corners of the forest.

The bright light of the Shadow Moon fell on the grass and spring flowers below the den and on the faces of the girls illuminating them both with a pale radiance that made them appear as forest spirits from tales of old.

The girls looked at one another, giggled, and scampered down the gentle slope of the hill. As they ran, swarms of fireflies, which are also called lightning bugs, rose from the grass and flew about their heads. The light of hundreds of fireflies flickered in the eyes of the two small racoons.

Giggling yet again, the girls began to chase the fireflies through the meadow.

After several moments they ran toward one another and jumped into each other's arms laughing and dancing and talking all at the same time. Rosie looked down at her girls and smiled.

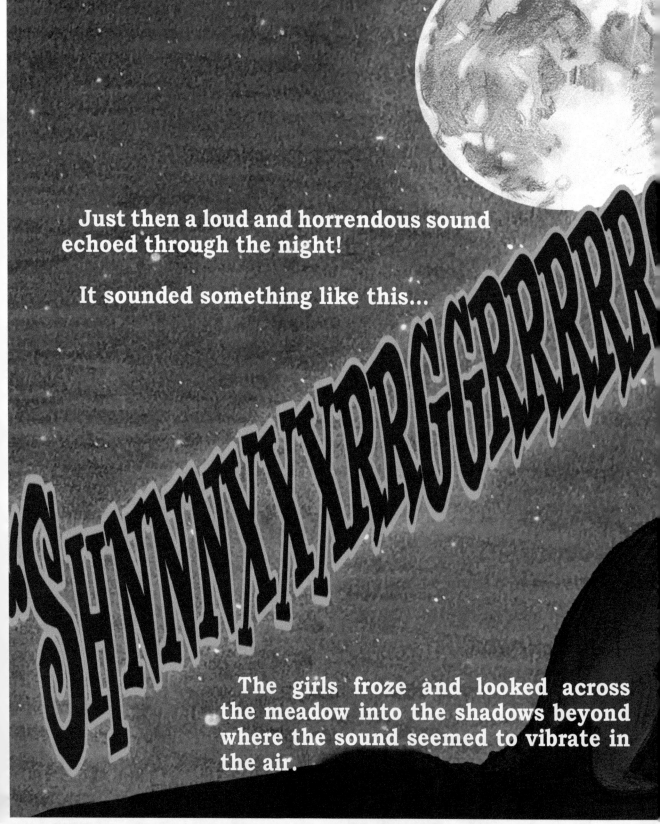

Just then a loud and horrendous sound echoed through the night!

It sounded something like this...

SHNNNXXYRRGGRRRRR

The girls froze and looked across the meadow into the shadows beyond where the sound seemed to vibrate in the air.

MMMMMMMMMMM!

Then, they looked up the hill at their mother who was standing at the entrance to the den.

Suddenly, the girls bolted back up the slope and into the safety of their mother's arms.

"What was that?" asked Sal.
"Was it a dragon?" asked Molly.
"Or a monster?"
"Or a..."

"Oh girls," said Rosie with a laugh. "Everything is all right! That's just Bartleby snoring!"

"He's a bear," said Rosie. "And he is still in his deep winter sleep. Come on, I'll show you where he lives."

She led the girls across the meadow into the deep shadows on the far side of the hill. They soon came to the entrance to a large cave, and, coming from the cave, the girls heard a sound that wasn't so scary this time.

"You see?" said their mother. "It's just Bartleby the bear. He will be waking up from his hibernation soon and I will introduce you to him."

"Come on girls," said Rosie with a twinkle in her eye. "Let's take a walk."

As they walked, she talked to Molly and Sal about their home in the mountains. She told them stories about the earth and the rocks and the flowers and the trees.

She continued talking to them as she led them past the berry patch and around the old fallen tree that had come down in a storm long ago. They walked on the forest path along the cliff top above the deep dark pool and to the top of the waterfall and beyond. And, as they walked, Molly and Sal listened and learned.

Finally, Rosie led her girls to a high mountain clearing far above the river where they took a rest on the ground and gazed up at the sky.

"Look at the stars girls," said Rosie, "and the moon. We call it Shadow Moon because it is so bright, especially on a night like tonight with no clouds in the sky."

"Look," she said. "You can see your shadow on the ground behind you."

And the girls looked behind themselves and discovered their shadows, which, of course, had been there all along. They were delighted by the discovery and began to chase each other's shadows giggling the whole time.

Rosie gathered the girls and led them back to the river and on to the path leading to the waterfall. As they walked, she told them about the many faces of the moon and the movement of the stars and the sun's journey through the sky.

She told them about clouds and rain and storms and snow. She taught them about the hot days of summer and the cold nights of winter.

She told them the many secrets of their home that they would need to know to grow and thrive in the years to come.

On their walk down the river, Rosie showed her girls how to listen, to really listen to the night. She taught them to pay attention to the world around them. And, as the girls were growing hungry, she taught them how to forage for food along the path.

After gathering small spring berries and pine nuts and tender leaves from plants that Rosie pointed out, they walked down the zigzag path to the river. There she taught the girls how to wash their food in the water by Big Red Rock.

After they ate, she showed them how to clean their paws and how to groom themselves, especially the mask around their eyes and the rings of their tails.

Rosie then told the girls about the other animals that lived with them in the mountains. She told them about Webster and Miss Ophelia and Kit and Theo and Peter the porcupine and Torrie the turtle and even Otto the grumpy badger who lived not far away by the shore of a lake. She told them about the many other animals who lived in the mountains.

She even told them about the people who often visited the cabin across the road from the river.

Finally, Rosie looked at her girls and asked, "Do you have any questions?"

"Oh yes, Mama," said Sal.
"We've got quite a lot," said Molly.
"Why does the moon move across the sky?"
"How does the river flow?"
"What is the deep dark pool?"
"Why do we only come out at night?"
"Why do we wash our food?"
"Where does the sun go at night?"
"Why does Bartleby snore so loudly?"
"Who are the people who stay in the cabin?"
"What is snow?"
"What is rain?"
"What are the stars?"
"Yes, what are the stars?"

Rosie listened to those questions and many, many more as they sat there on the river bank bathed in the moon's glow. She tried to answer each question as best she could. After listening to the last questions about the stars Rosie said, "I know just who to ask about that. Follow me girls."

She led them up the zigzag path to the meadow by the gazebo. She led them past the chair-table-chair and across the dirt road and into the clearing by the cabin. She led them to the base of a huge old growth pine framed against the fading light of the setting Shadow Moon.

There, sitting on a lower branch of the tree, was a large grey owl whose round unblinking eyes looked down at them all.

"Good evening Webster," said Rosie. "These are my girls Molly and Sal."

"Hello Molly. Hello Sal," said the owl. "Your mother has told me all about you. I'm very happy to meet you."

"Hello," said Molly. "You're an owl."

"Mama has told us all about you too," said Sal.

"She has told us a lot of things."

"But one thing we really wanted to know."

"What are the stars?"

"What a delightful question," said Webster. "Let me tell you a story that will help you understand."

"Our story begins," said Webster, "with this very tree."

The girls looked up at the tree and at Webster and their eyes grew wide.

"You see," continued Webster, "this tree has been here for as long as anyone can recall. I remember my father telling me stories about it that he learned from his father who learned from his father and so on. The tree has been a guardian and a friend to us all for many, many years."

"Legend has it that long ago when the tree was young it grew strong and sturdy and tall. Over time, its upper branches grew so tall that they brushed against the belly of the sky. And, when the wind blew, the top branches tickled the sky!"

"Now you girls know when your belly is tickled you can't help but begin to laugh! And that is just what the sky did! It laughed and laughed and its belly jiggled and shook, and suddenly some of the branches of the tree poked through the belly of the sky, letting the light from above shine through. Night after night this happened."

"And that, my dears," said Webster, "is how the stars were born."

"Oh my," said Sal rubbing her eyes.
"How wonderful," said Molly with a yawn.

"Well," said Webster, "it looks like you girls have had enough stories for tonight. You had better get them home to bed Rosie."

So, Rosie collected the very tired girls. They all said goodnight to Webster and began the walk back to their den. As they reached their meadow, Rosie looked across the hill and noticed that Bartleby had emerged from his long winter sleep and was sitting on a rock outside of his cave.

"Come on girls," said Rosie. "I want to introduce you to Bartleby."

They crossed the meadow to Bartleby's cave where they found him rubbing his eyes with one paw while scratching his belly with the other.

"Hello Rosie," said Bartleby with a great yawn. "Is it time to get up?"

"Yes it is," chuckled Rosie. "Girls, this is our friend Bartleby."

Sal and Molly looked at Bartleby and each other and then, giggling, they ran to the sleepy old bear. They both hugged him as hard as they could saying....

"Hello Bartleby!"
"I'm Molly!"
"And I'm Sal!"
"We heard you snoring earlier tonight!"
"It was really scary at first."
"But then it was kind of funny."
"We're very happy to meet you!"

And they hugged him again.

Bartleby rested a huge paw on each girl and said, "I'm happy to meet you too." And then he hugged them back really quite gently.

"We'd better go girls," said Rosie. "Bartleby needs to wake up and we need to get you to bed." Hugs were given again and goodbyes were said.

As the three racoons crossed the meadow to their den they all noticed that the Shadow Moon was setting behind the mountains to the northwest and that the pink blush of dawn was starting to color the sky to the east.

After they reached the den Rosie kissed the girls and got them settled down for a good day's sleep. She heard them say...

"That was the best night ever."
"I know. I can't wait for tomorrow night."

And they both fell fast asleep.

The End

IF YOU ENJOYED

THE

SHADOW MOON

CHECK OUT THE BOOK THAT STARTED IT ALL:

Dylan loves his time at the cabin each year. He loves the mountains, and the river, and the wildlife, and the adventures. Most of all though, he loves spending time with his Papa. And the best times with Papa are spent hearing stories each night under The Story Tree.

From Bartleby the bear's incredible itch, to Theo the fish's scary first day at a new school, Dylan hears stories under the Story Tree that are both timely and entertaining.

Available anywhere books are sold.
Or, contact:

The Get It Factory
Publishing House

www.thegetitfactory.com

CPSIA information can be obtained
at www.ICGtesting.com
Printed in the USA
LVHW061553070921
697218LV00003B/363